To Jake. You've lived a lifetime of stories about bears—
from sleeping bears in Michigan to blueberry-eating bears of northern Minnesota.
You are and will always be my favorite cub.

—K. J. W.

For my dear old Mum who is always there for us, and as ever Tiziana, my adorable wife.

—J. B. B.

Sleeping Bear Press™

2395 South Huron Parkway, Suite 200
Ann Arbor, MI 48104
www.sleepingbearpress.com

© 2010 Sleeping Bear Press

Printed and bound in the United States.

10 9 8 7 6

Library of Congress Cataloging-in-Publication Data

Wargin, Kathy-jo.
Scare a bear / written by Kathy-jo Wargin ; illustrated by John Bendall-Brunello. — 1st ed.
p. cm.
Summary: In rhyming text, the reader is asked how to scare a bear if one wanders into camp, or
wants to go for a boat ride, or stays for supper.
ISBN 978-1-58536-430-5
[1. Stories in rhyme. 2. Bears—Fiction. 3. Camping—Fiction.] I. Bendall-Brunello, John, ill. II. Title.
PZ8.3.W2172Sc 2010
[E]—dc22
2009037416

Scare a Bear

Kathy-jo Wargin

Illustrated by

John Bendall-Brunello

Sleeping Bear Press™

PUBLISHER

Would you bang
pots and pans?
Would you rattle some cans?
Would you shout?
Would you yell?

Would you ring
a loud **bell**?

Would you make a strange face and a big scary **pose?**

Would you shout,
"I declare, it's a **bear**!
Please **beware**!"

What if that **bear**
isn't easy to **scare**?

What if that bear
wants to go for a swim?
Would you holler and **hoot**?
Would you give him the **boot**?

Would you say,
    "You can't swim here.
            You don't have a **suit!**"

What if that bear
wants to go for a swim?

What if that bear wants
to fish from your boat?
Do you think he would **fit**?
Would you tell him to **sit**?
Would you share your **pole**

and your best fishing **hole**?
Do you think he would **squirm**
if you showed him a **worm**?
What if that bear
wants to fish from your boat?

What if that bear starts to beg
for some dinner?
Would you share your **peas**?
Do you think he'll say **please**?
Would you give him a **dish**
with a big tasty
fish?

What if that bear starts to beg for some dinner?

What if that bear
sits down by the fire?

Would you share your seat?
Would you make him a treat?

Would you tell him you think he's had too much to **eat**?

Now what if that bear wants to sleep overnight?

KERPLUNK!

Would you start to giggle
if he starts to wiggle?

What if he snores?
Would you send him outdoors?

If he climbed in your bunk,
would the bed go kerplunk?

What if that bear wants to sleep overnight?

What if that bear will not leave the next morning?
Would you give him a **map**
with a compass and **cap**?

Would you
tell him,
"Keep walking.
Don't stop
for a **nap!**"

Would you say, "My dear Bear,
there's no need for **stalling**.
It's time to go home. Your mother is **calling!**"

What if that bear will not leave in the morning? Then call the ranger.

I know what he'll **say**.

"This bear cannot **stay**. You must scare him **away**."